A Note for Parents and Teachers

A focus on phonics helps beginning readers gain skill and confidence with reading. Each story in the Bright Owl Books series highlights one vowel sound— for *Rat Attack*, it's the short "a" sound. At the end of the book, you'll find two Story Starters, just for fun. Story Starters are open-ended questions that can be used as a jumping-off place for conversation, storytelling, and imaginative writing.

At Kane Press, we believe the most important part of any reading program is the shared experience of a good story. We hope you'll enjoy *Rat Attack* with a child you love!

Library of Congress Cataloging-in-Publication Data
Names: Coxe, Molly, author, illustrator.
Title: Rat attack / by Molly Coxe.
Description: First Kane Press edition. | New York : Kane Press, [2018] | Series: Bright owl books | "Originally published in different form by BraveMouse Books in 2014." | Summary: "Gran is making jam but rats want the jam and attack in this easy-to-read book featuring the short 'a' sound"—Provided by publisher.
Identifiers: LCCN 2017054184| ISBN 9781575659732 (pbk) | ISBN 9781575659725 (reinforced library binding) | ISBN 9781575659749 (ebook)
Subjects: | CYAC: Jam—Fiction. | Mice—Fiction. | Rats—Fiction. | Stealing—Fiction.
Classification: LCC PZ7.C839424 Rat 2018 | DDC [E]—dc23
LC record available at https://lccn.loc.gov/2017054184

10 9 8 7 6 5 4 3 2 1

Printed in China

Book Design: Michelle Martinez

Bright Owl Books is a trademark of Kane Press, Inc.

Visit us online at
www.kanepress.com

 Like us on Facebook
facebook.com/kanepress

 Follow us on Twitter
@KanePress

RAT ATTACK

by Molly Coxe

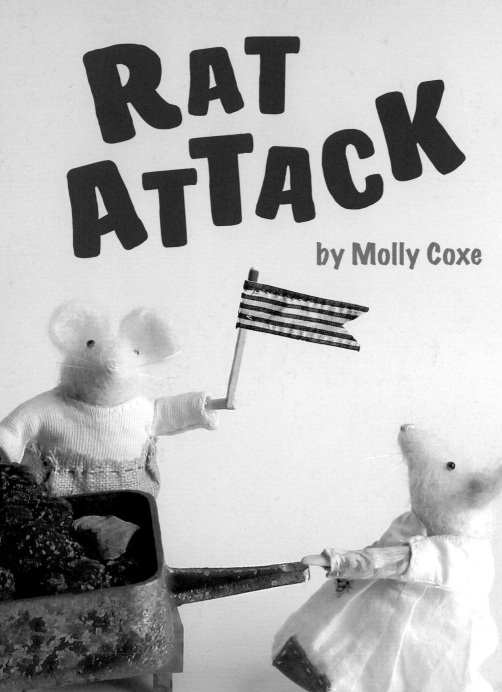

Kane Press • New York

Gram is making jam for Ann, Fran, and Stan.

She hears a tap.
"Who's that?"
asks Gram.

"I am a bandit, ma'am.
Hand over the jam."

"You are not a bandit,"
 says Gram.
"You are Nat the rat.
 Scat, Nat!"

Gram is making jam.
She hears a tap.
"Who's that?" asks Gram.

"I am a giant!
Fee fi fo fum!
Give me jam
to fill my tum."

"You are not a giant,"
says Gram.
"You are Pat the rat.
Scat, Pat!"

Gram is making jam.
She hears a tap.
"Who's that?" asks Gram.

"I am a magician!
Put some jam in here.
I will make it disappear!"

"You are not a magician,"
says Gram.
"You are Matt the rat.
Scat, Matt!"

Gram is making jam.
She hears a tap.
"Who's that?" asks Gram.

"This is a rat attack!"
say Nat, Pat, and Matt.

"Ann, Fran, Stan, come fast!"
says Gram.

"The rats are stealing the jam!"
says Gram.

"We have a plan,"
say Ann, Fran, and Stan.

The rats hear a tap.
"Who's that?" ask the rats.

"This is a cat attack!"
say Ann, Fran,
and Stan.

The rats scat.
"Anyone for jam?" asks Gram.
"Yes, ma'am!"
say Ann, Fran, and Stan.

The End

Story Starters

The rats are mad.
What is their plan?

Ann has a tall ladder.
What is at the top?